The Young Scientist Book of ELECTRICITY

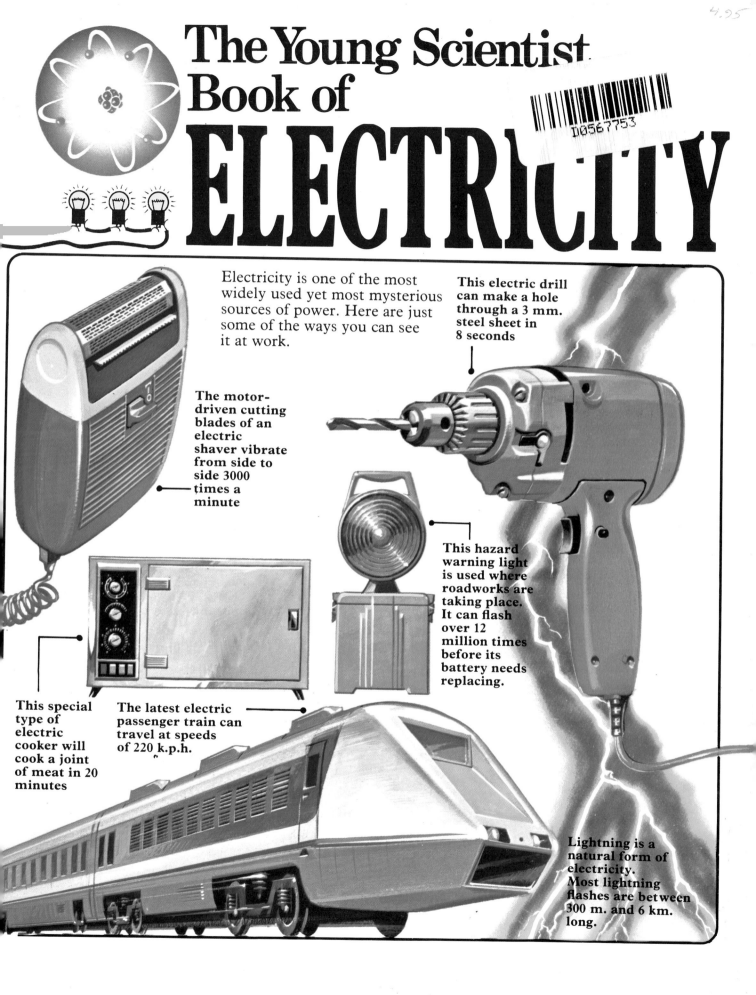

Electricity is one of the most widely used yet most mysterious sources of power. Here are just some of the ways you can see it at work.

This electric drill can make a hole through a 3 mm. steel sheet in 8 seconds

The motor-driven cutting blades of an electric shaver vibrate from side to side 3000 times a minute

This hazard warning light is used where roadworks are taking place. It can flash over 12 million times before its battery needs replacing.

This special type of electric cooker will cook a joint of meat in 20 minutes

The latest electric passenger train can travel at speeds of 220 k.p.h.

Lightning is a natural form of electricity. Most lightning flashes are between 300 m. and 6 km. long.

CREDITS

Written by
Philip Chapman
Art and editorial direction
David Jefferis
Educational adviser
Frank Blackwell

Illustrators
Roland Berry
Sydney Cornford
Malcolm English
Phil Green
John Hutchinson
Malcolm McGregor
Michael Roffe

Acknowledgements
We wish to thank the following individuals and organizations for their assistance and for making available material in their collections.
British Post Office
Brook Motors Ltd.
Central Electricity Generating Board

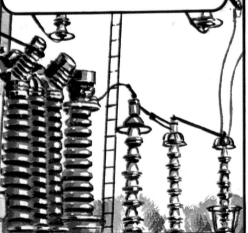

On the cover: a generator makes million-volt sparks

On this page: the transformer in a power station

THE EXPERIMENTS

All the experiments in this book are absolutely safe if you always use a 4.5 volt battery.
NEVER play with electricity from the mains.

Here is a list of equipment you will need.

General equipment

Four 6 volt bulbs in bulbholders
Two 4.5 volt batteries with screw-down connections
About 5 m. of connecting wire
Sticky tape
Scissors
Glue
Compass
15 m. of fine insulated wire
Paper clips
12 cm. long nail
Wire cutters
Two magnets
Plasticine

For special experiments

Current detector (p. 13):
Saucer
Water
Small cork
Needle

Motor (p. 15):
15 × 17 cm. sheet of balsa wood
50 cm. of 5 × 5 mm. balsa wood strip
Balsa cement
Ten 3 cm. long pins
15 cm. long knitting needle
Two drawing pins

The battery we have chosen for all the experiments in this book supplies electricity at 4.5 volts. Not all batteries supplying this voltage look the same, so get ones looking like either of the two shown below.

The battery with screw-on terminals is best because you can fix the wires very easily. You can use the battery with springy terminals but you will have to wind the wires onto them.

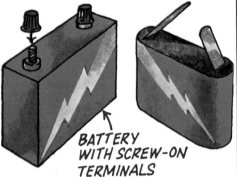

BATTERY WITH SCREW-ON TERMINALS

Large cork
Two horseshoe magnets
Two aluminium milk bottle tops

Turbine (p. 21):
15 cm. long knitting needle
Sheet of stiff paper about 10 cm. × 10 cm.

Telegraph set (p. 26):
Sheet of cooking foil
Length of 3-core cable
Large sheet of cardboard

WEIGHTS AND MEASURES

All the weights and measures used in this book are metric. This list gives some equivalents in Imperial measures.

mm. = millimetre
(1 inch = 25.4 mm.)

cm. = centimetre
(1 inch = 2.54 cm.)

m. = metre
(1 yard = 0.91 m.)

km. = kilometre
(1 mile = 1.6 km.)

k.p.h. = kilometres per hour
(100 m.p.h. = 160 k.p.h.)

sq. km. = square kilometre
(1 square mile = 2.59 sq. km.)

kg. = kilogram
(1 pound = 0.45 kg.)

A tonne is 1000 kg.
(1 ton = 1.02 tonnes)

1 litre is 1.76 pints

M means one million
(1 MW = one million watts)

k means 1000
(1 kW. = 1000 watts)

°C. = degrees Centigrade
(Water freezes at 0°C. and boils at 100°C.)

The Young Scientist Book of ELECTRICITY

ABOUT THIS BOOK

Do you know why an electric light bulb shines or how a battery works? Have you ever wondered how electricity is made in a power station or how an electric motor works?

This book explains in simple terms what electricity is, and how it works and how we use it. It tells the story of how electricity is made, transmitted around the country, and finally reaches our homes, offices and factories.

A series of safe and simple experiments easily carried out on the kitchen table shows you how to construct simple circuits, including working models of an electromagnet, an electric motor and a two-way telegraph system.

CONTENTS

INSIDE THE ATOM

Everything is made up of atoms. The air you breathe, the pages of this book, your own body—all are built up from millions of invisibly small atoms. They are so small that ten million of them lined up side by side would measure only one millimetre!

At the centre of each atom is a nucleus containing tiny particles called protons. Even smaller particles called electrons move round the nucleus. They orbit round the nucleus like planets round the Sun, and there are always as many electrons as protons.

Each electron has a negative electric charge; each proton has a positive electric charge.

This ⊖ sign means negative and this ⊕ sign means positive.

The atom

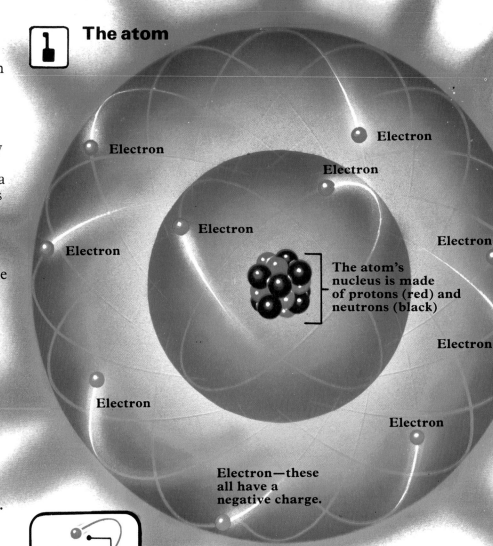

The atom's nucleus is made of protons (red) and neutrons (black)

Electron—these all have a negative charge.

▶ Hydrogen is the simplest atom. It has only one proton and one electron. All the other atoms are more complicated. They have other particles called neutrons, but these have no electric charge at all. The big picture shows you the important parts of an atom.

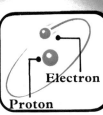

Electron

Proton

Electric circuits

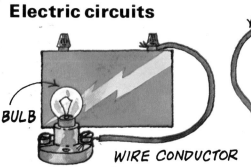

BULB

WIRE CONDUCTOR

SECOND WIRE WILL ACT AS A RETURN PATH

BULB GLOWS

▲ To light a bulb using a supply of electricity from a battery, the bulb must be connected to the battery. An electrical conductor such as a wire provides an easy path for the electrons to follow.

▲ But simply connecting a single wire from the battery to the bulb will not light it. A second wire must be connected to the battery's other terminal. This makes a path for the electrons to flow back to the battery.

▲ This unbroken path is called a circuit. The second wire has completed the circuit, and the bulb lights up. The electrons flow through the bulb but are not used up in it. They pass through and return to the battery.

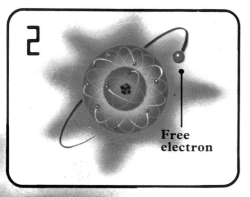

2

Free electron

▲ An electrical conductor is something that allows electricity to pass through it easily. A good conductor has one 'free' electron orbiting outside the others. It can be separated from its atom.

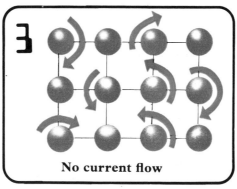

3

No current flow

▲ In metals, the atoms form a regular pattern. This gives metals their strength. The free electrons do not orbit round their own atoms, but can wander from atom to atom through the metal. The red arrows above show them moving.

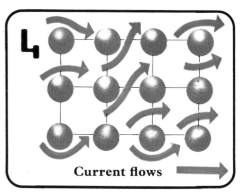

4

Current flows

▲ When a metal wire is connected to a battery, the free electrons in the wire start to drift from one end to the other, passing from atom to atom. This drift of electrons is called an electric current.

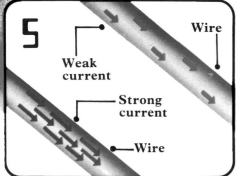

5

Wire

Weak current

Strong current

Wire

▲ The strength of an electric current flowing in a wire depends on the number of free electrons passing along it. Lots of free electrons mean a strong current, a few mean a weak current is flowing.

6

Filament

▲ When you switch on a light in your home, this lets the electric current flow through the bulb. About 3 million million million free electrons are passing through the filament in the bulb every second!

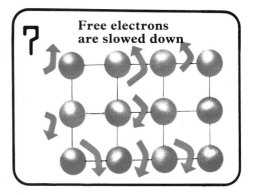

7

Free electrons are slowed down

▲ Free electrons do not pass along a wire smoothly. They bump into the atoms of the wire and their progress is slowed down. This slowing-down effect is called resistance. The better the conductor, the lower its resistance.

Instant electricity

The free electrons drifting along a wire move quite slowly—only a few millimetres a second. This mini-experiment shows you why you do not have to wait when you turn on an electricity supply.

Get some marbles and line them up between two books. Push the left-hand marble a little way to the right. See how all the other marbles move as well, even at the far end. Like marbles, electrons all begin to move at the same time, but they do so only when their circuit is completed—so they have a return path back to the battery.

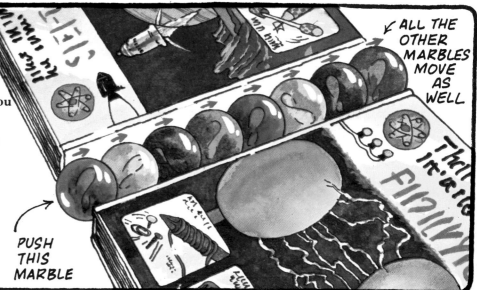

ALL THE OTHER MARBLES MOVE AS WELL

PUSH THIS MARBLE

NATURE'S ELECTRICITY

A lightning storm is one of nature's most dramatic shows of strength. Flashes of electricity leap down from thunderclouds in the sky.

Although men have known about thunderstorms for thousands of years, exactly what causes them is still not very clear.

Scientists say that lightning is the releasing of electricity that has built up inside the clouds. It is probably like the electricity that is built up when you comb your hair on a warm dry day. You can sometimes hear a crackling noise as the teeth of the comb pass the strands of hair.

Lightning conductors are strips of metal running down the side of a building. They provide an easy path for the electricity to follow and so keep the lightning away from the building itself.

Lightning will strike a tree rather than go direct to the ground because the tree gives the lightning an easier path to earth. Why? Because the tree-top is nearer to the cloud than the ground.

1 Making electricity with a comb

Things sometimes get charged with electricity just by rubbing. Have you ever felt a small shock when you touch a door knob after walking across a thick pile carpet? This is because electrons have been rubbed off the carpet and onto your body. This 'static' charge then escapes suddenly as you touch the door knob, and you feel a tingling shock.

Here are two experiments you can do to show the effects of static electricity.

▲ Comb your hair with a plastic comb. As the comb's teeth pass the strands of your hair, electrons are transferred across, and the comb becomes charged with static electricity. Make sure you comb your hair vigorously.

▲ Hold the comb a little way from some small scraps of paper. You will see the pieces of paper jump up to the comb and stick to it. The static electricity in the comb is attracting the pieces of paper.

Electricity may flash across between two clouds. This is the most common type of lightning. It appears as a bright flash across the sky.

Lightning strikes direct to the ground are quite rare. The lightning normally strikes a tree or building as these provide an easier path for the electricity to follow.

▲ The skin of an electric eel conceals hundreds of tiny cells all acting like miniature batteries. The cells charge up to a voltage of more than 600 volts which the eel then uses to stun its victim.

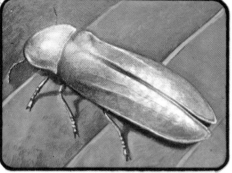

▲ Glow worms are light-producing beetles. Their pale yellowish-green glow is made by a chemical process in the rear part of their bodies. They can flash their lights in special rhythms to attract each other.

▲ Your own body is one of the most complicated electrical systems. All information from the senses—sight, sound, touch, taste and smell—is passed to the brain along nerve fibres. The information is passed along as an electric signal. This footballer's brain receives all the information needed for him to aim and kick the ball. His brain then sends out electric signals along nerve fibres to tell his muscles when and where to kick the ball.

PIECES OF PAPER FALL

▲ After a minute or two, the electricity in the comb leaks away through your body, and the scraps of paper will fall off. You can repeat the experiment if you comb your hair again to recharge it with static electricity.

SLOW AND STEADY FLOW

▲ Another static electricity trick is bending water. Turn on a water tap and adjust it carefully until a slow, steady stream of water is flowing. Comb your hair again and hold the comb near the stream of flowing water.

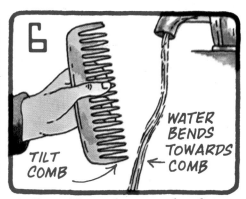

TILT COMB

WATER BENDS TOWARDS COMB

▲ You will see the water bend towards the tip of the comb. The static electricity in the comb is attracting the water towards it. Again the charge leaks away through your body. As it does so, the water flows normally again.

HOW BATTERIES WORK

Electric current is the movement of electrons through a wire. They won't travel along the wire by themselves, so a force is needed to push them along. This force is produced by a battery and is called the electromotive force.

The strength of the force is measured in volts, named after Alessandro Volta, the inventor of the first battery.

Batteries are not as powerful as the electricity supplied to our homes, but they can be carried about from place to place or used as an emergency supply during a power cut.

▲ In 1800, Count Volta, an Italian scientist, made the first battery. A supply of electric current was now available to experimenters who until then had used static electricity which lasts for only a few seconds at a time.

▲ The voltaic pile, as Volta's battery came to be known, was made of lots of silver and zinc discs separated by damp fabric pads. The electric current made by the voltaic pile could be used for lots of long-lasting experiments.

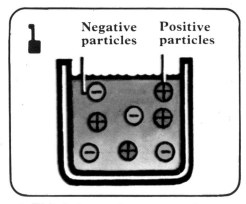

Negative particles **Positive particles**

▲ This is how a battery works. It is made of lots of cells and one of them is shown above. In the cell is a liquid called the electrolyte. It is made of billions of positive and negative particles.

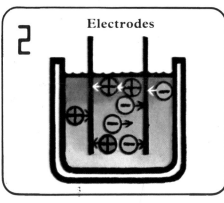

Electrodes

▲ Two rods made of different materials are submerged in the electrolyte in each cell. These are called electrodes. A chemical reaction in the electrolyte sends positive particles to one electrode, negative particles to the other.

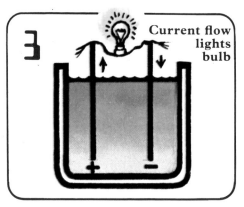

Current flow lights bulb

▲ When a wire is connected to the two electrodes, current flows along the wire. This can be used to light a bulb like the one shown above. When the chemicals in the cell are used up, the current stops flowing.

Dry cells

Liquids can easily spill out so special dry batteries are made for things like torches. There are still two electrodes, the carbon rod and the zinc case, but the cell has a paste electrolyte sealed into its leakproof case.

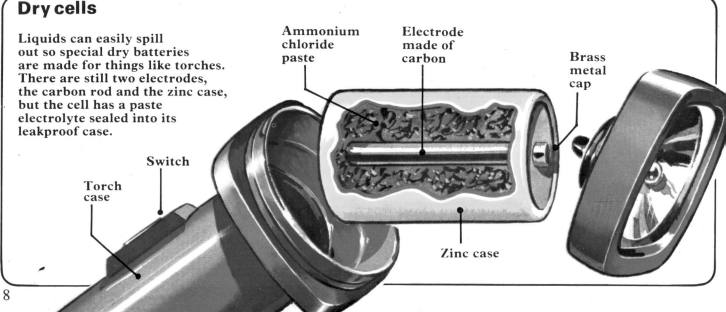

Ammonium chloride paste

Electrode made of carbon

Brass metal cap

Switch

Torch case

Zinc case

8

Rechargeable power for the motor car

A modern car uses many small electrical machines: starter motor, heater motor and fan. They would soon wear out an ordinary battery so special car batteries are made. These are designed so that they can be recharged with electricity.

A small electric generator is driven by the car engine. The power it produces when the engine is running is fed back into the battery to replace that used by the starter motor in starting the car.

Battery

Electric generator

Lights

Lights

Heater motor

Starter motor

This picture shows just some of the things in a car which use up the battery's electricity supply. You can also see the generator which recharges the battery. Almost all car batteries provide a 12 volt power supply.

Non-polluting power of the future

Two electric cars draw up at 1997's clean version of our filling station. The driver on the right has just inserted his credit card (1). Robot machinery underground slots in a newly charged battery module (2) under the driving compartment. The old battery is pushed out of the other side of the car by the new module. It passes into the automatic receiving bay (3) to go for recharging. Once recharged, (4) it glides along a conveyor belt to be used again (5). A 30 second 'fill-up' gives another 1000 km. driving.

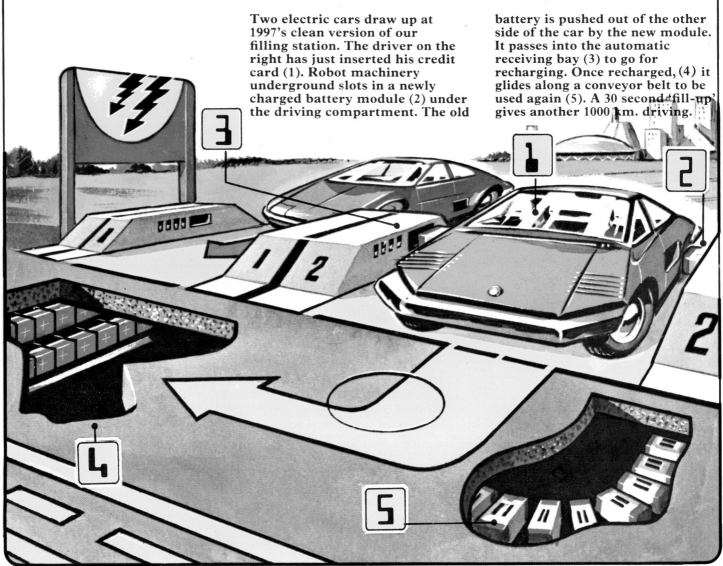

TURNING POWER INTO LIGHT

American inventor Thomas Edison

Thomas Edison produced the first electric light bulb in 1879. He sealed a fine cotton thread into a glass bulb. After pumping out the air he saw that the thread glowed brightly when a current was passed through it.

The thread had a high resistance because it was so fine. The electrons passing through it kept bumping into the atoms of the thread. This heated it up so much that it glowed white hot.

If you look at a new light bulb in its cardboard packet, you will see a number—60W or 100W. This tells you how much power the bulb uses and how brightly it glows. The bigger the number the brighter the glow. The W stands for watt, the unit of power named after James Watt the Scottish inventor.

Length and resistance

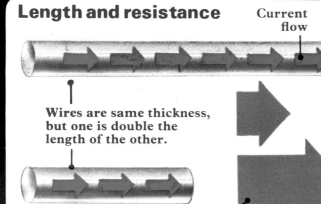

Current flow

Wires are same thickness, but one is double the length of the other.

Shorter wire—less resistance, so more current.

Good conductors of electricity allow electrons to flow easily. Sometimes they bump into atoms in the wire. This slows them down. The braking effect is called the wire's resistance. Halving the length of the wire halves the resistance.

Width and resistance

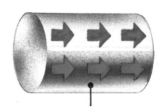

Wires are the same length, but one is twice as thick as the other.

Thick wire—less resistance, so more current.

A thick wire has a lower resistance than a thin wire. There is a greater area of wire for the electrons to pass through. It is like a wide three-lane motorway that can carry far more traffic than a narrow single-lane country road.

Current and resistance

BULB GLOWS BRIGHTLY

DIM GLOW

4.5

4.5

▲ Connect a wire from the ⊕ terminal of a battery to a bulbholder terminal. Then wire the other bulbholder terminal to the ⊖ of the battery. The battery forces current round the wire and through the bulb.

▲ Now connect up the second bulb to the first and complete the circuit to the battery. The bulbs glow less brightly now. By connecting up the second bulb you have doubled the resistance so less current flows.

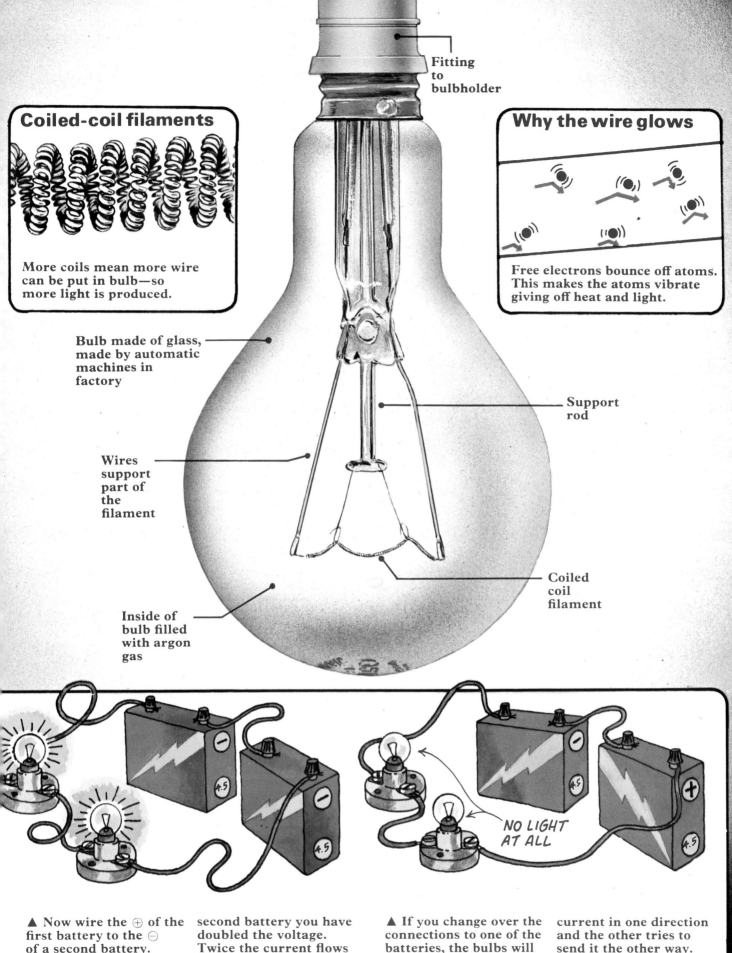

Coiled-coil filaments

More coils mean more wire can be put in bulb—so more light is produced.

Fitting to bulbholder

Why the wire glows

Free electrons bounce off atoms. This makes the atoms vibrate giving off heat and light.

Bulb made of glass, made by automatic machines in factory

Support rod

Wires support part of the filament

Inside of bulb filled with argon gas

Coiled coil filament

NO LIGHT AT ALL

▲ Now wire the ⊕ of the first battery to the ⊖ of a second battery. The bulbs glow brightly again. By connecting the second battery you have doubled the voltage. Twice the current flows and the bulbs shine brightly again.

▲ If you change over the connections to one of the batteries, the bulbs will not light up. The first battery tries to send current in one direction and the other tries to send it the other way. The result is no current flow at all.

11

MAGNETISM AND ELECTRICITY

Pulley

Electromagnet

Thick power cable

Boom of scrapyard crane

The electromagnet has just been switched off—its load is falling down to the ground.

Magnetism has been known for thousands of years, and scientists have puzzled over it for just as long. The strange invisible force that attracts pieces of iron and steel to a magnet is still not fully understood.

A magnet affects only certain materials, and then only when they are close to it. They must be within its magnetic field.

Magnetism has been put to good use. Giant electromagnets like the one above lift very heavy loads, and for centuries sailors have used the compass for navigation.

Needle points north

▲ A compass needle is a small magnet, and it always points to the Earth's north pole. All magnets are therefore said to have magnetic poles. The north-seeking pole is the north pole and the other is the south pole.

Unlike poles attract

Like poles repel

▲ When a pair of magnets are placed close together, they attract one another if a north pole faces a south pole. Two north poles or two south poles face to face repel one another.

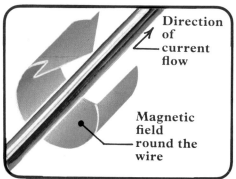

Direction of current flow

Magnetic field round the wire

▲ When a wire carries an electric current, a magnetic field is produced round the wire. The field is present along the whole length of the wire, and if the current is increased the field gets stronger.

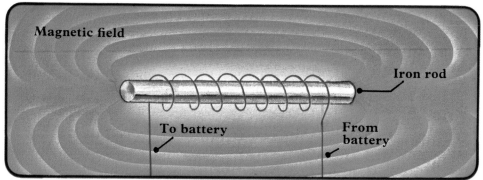

Magnetic field

Iron rod

To battery

From battery

▲ Simple and small magnets like horseshoe-shaped ones are not very powerful. A stronger magnet is produced when a coil of wire is wound round an iron bar. As soon as the current is switched on the bar becomes a very powerful magnet that can be switched off simply by stopping the current flow. Giant electromagnets like the one above are used in scrap metal yards and lift huge loads of metal at a time.

Make an electromagnet

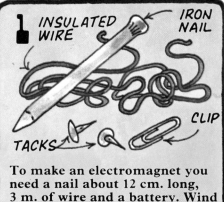

1 INSULATED WIRE — IRON NAIL — TACKS — CLIP

To make an electromagnet you need a nail about 12 cm. long, 3 m. of wire and a battery. Wind 60 turns of wire around the nail. Put sticky tape on to stop it unwinding.

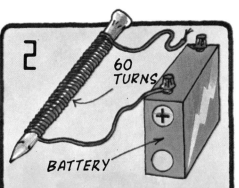

2 60 TURNS — BATTERY

Remove about 2 cm. of the plastic insulation from each loose end of the wire. Wind one end of the bare wire around the $\oplus$ terminal of the battery. Make sure that the wire will not slip.

3 NAIL PICKS UP TACKS AND CLIPS — WIRES TO BATTERY

Touch the other end of the wire onto the $\ominus$ terminal of the battery. The electromagnet will now pick up nails, paperclips and other small objects with iron in them.

Detect electric currents

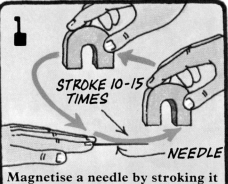

1 STROKE 10-15 TIMES — NEEDLE

Magnetise a needle by stroking it with a magnet. Make sure the return path of the magnet is well away from the needle, otherwise the needle will be very poorly magnetised.

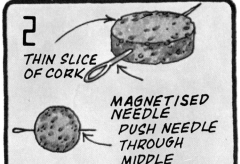

2 THIN SLICE OF CORK — MAGNETISED NEEDLE — PUSH NEEDLE THROUGH MIDDLE

Cut a slice of cork about 1 cm. thick. Push the needle through the cork, making sure it passes through the centre so that it will float properly when you put it into a dish of water.

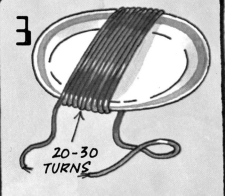

3 20-30 TURNS

Now wind 20 to 30 turns of wire around the dish. Keep the wire in place with sticky tape. Place the dish well away from electrical appliances, and pour in enough water to float the cork.

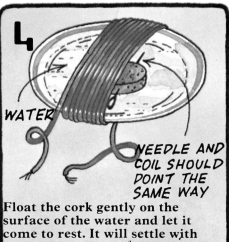

4 WATER — NEEDLE AND COIL SHOULD POINT THE SAME WAY

Float the cork gently on the surface of the water and let it come to rest. It will settle with one end pointing northwards. The needle must be able to float without scraping against the wire.

5 SCREW WIRE TO TERMINAL — TOUCH WIRE TO TERMINAL — NEEDLE KICKS WHEN CIRCUIT IS COMPLETED

Remove 2 cm. of insulation from the ends of the wire. Connect one end to the $\ominus$ terminal of the battery. Touch the other wire to the $\oplus$ terminal. The needle will give a 'kick' and spin round.

This is because the coil round the dish produces a magnetic field when a current flows through it. The needle then turns round to line itself up with this field.

THE ELECTRIC MOTOR

English scientist Michael Faraday invented the first electric motor in 1831. He could hardly have known at the time just how revolutionary this discovery would turn out to be.

Now industry all over the world uses electric motors to make everything from pins to spacecraft.

Motors drive inter-city and underground trains, and kitchens throughout the world would come to a halt without motors to drive food mixers, refrigerators, washing machines and other gadgets.

Inside an electric motor

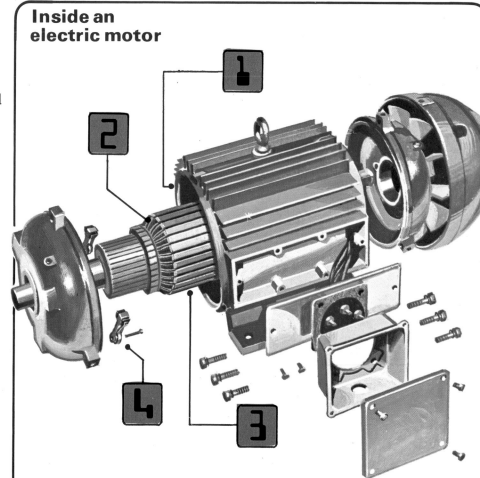

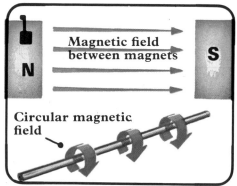

▲ The force that makes an electric motor turn round is produced when two magnetic fields meet. The first is the field between two magnetic poles and the second is the one round a wire carrying an electric current.

In the motor shown here, the magnetic field is produced by electromagnets (1), the coils carrying the current (2) are wound round the armature (3). The current goes to the coils through brushes (4).

In the model opposite, the magnetic field is produced by two horseshoe magnets, the armature is made from coils wound round a cork, and the current is passed to them using milk bottle tops as brushes.

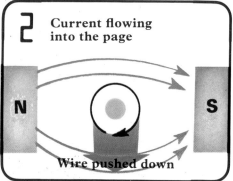

2 Current flowing into the page

▲ In an electric motor, a wire is put between two magnets. (The circle in the picture above is an end-on view of the wire.) When the current is flowing along the wire, into the page, the wire is pushed downwards.

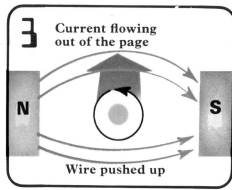

3 Current flowing out of the page

▲ If the current in the wire is travelling the other way—out of the page in this picture—the push on the wire changes as well. The wire is now pushed upwards instead of downwards.

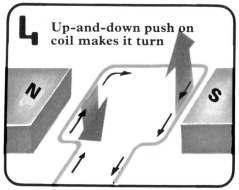

4 Up-and-down push on coil makes it turn

▲ Using a coil of wire means that the current flows first into, then out of, the page. So one part of the wire is pushed downwards and the other pushed upwards. Putting the coil on a shaft lets it spin round.

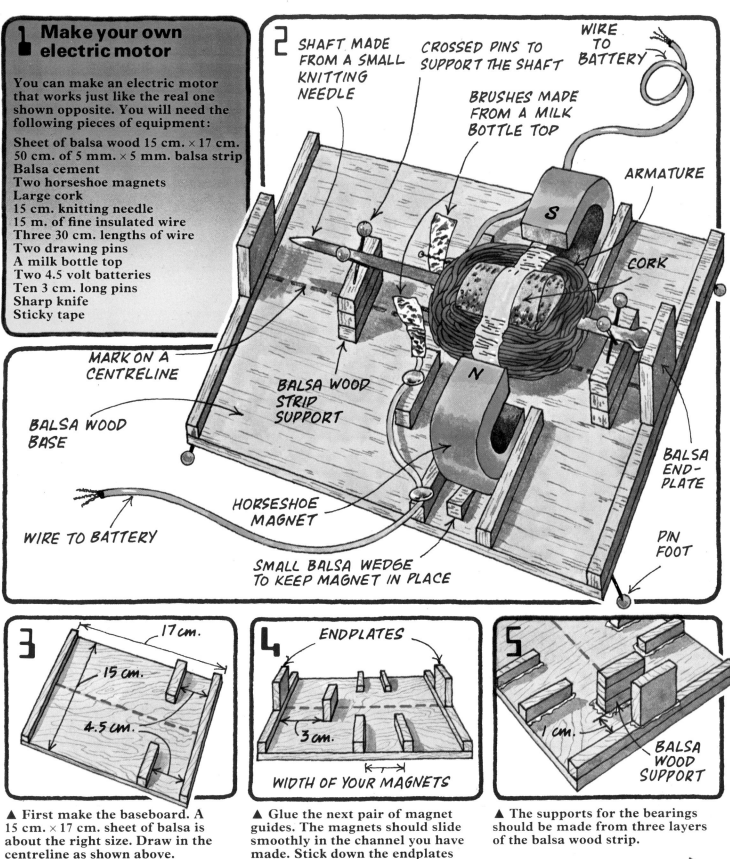

1 Make your own electric motor

You can make an electric motor that works just like the real one shown opposite. You will need the following pieces of equipment:

Sheet of balsa wood 15 cm. × 17 cm.
50 cm. of 5 mm. × 5 mm. balsa strip
Balsa cement
Two horseshoe magnets
Large cork
15 cm. knitting needle
15 m. of fine insulated wire
Three 30 cm. lengths of wire
Two drawing pins
A milk bottle top
Two 4.5 volt batteries
Ten 3 cm. long pins
Sharp knife
Sticky tape

2

SHAFT MADE FROM A SMALL KNITTING NEEDLE

CROSSED PINS TO SUPPORT THE SHAFT

WIRE TO BATTERY

BRUSHES MADE FROM A MILK BOTTLE TOP

ARMATURE

S

CORK

N

MARK ON A CENTRELINE

BALSA WOOD STRIP SUPPORT

BALSA WOOD BASE

WIRE TO BATTERY

HORSESHOE MAGNET

SMALL BALSA WEDGE TO KEEP MAGNET IN PLACE

BALSA END-PLATE

PIN FOOT

3

17 cm.

15 cm.

4.5 cm.

▲ First make the baseboard. A 15 cm. × 17 cm. sheet of balsa is about the right size. Draw in the centreline as shown above. Glue down the end strips and the first two magnet guides 4.5 cm. from one end of the baseboard.

4

ENDPLATES

3 cm.

WIDTH OF YOUR MAGNETS

▲ Glue the next pair of magnet guides. The magnets should slide smoothly in the channel you have made. Stick down the endplates across the centreline. These will keep the motor in place when it goes round.

5

1 cm.

BALSA WOOD SUPPORT

▲ The supports for the bearings should be made from three layers of the balsa wood strip.

Continued next page →

15

Make your own electric motor
continued from p.15

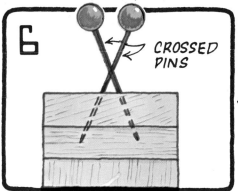

6 CROSSED PINS

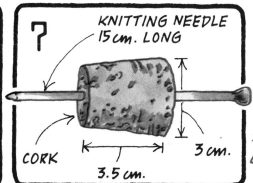

7 KNITTING NEEDLE 15 cm. LONG
CORK
3.5 cm.
3 cm.

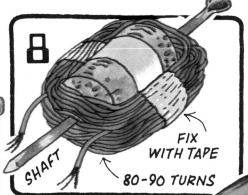

8 SHAFT
FIX WITH TAPE
80-90 TURNS

▲ Use crossed pins to support the armature shaft. They do not need plastic ends like the ones shown, but they should be at least 3 cm. long. Push them very firmly into the wood, so they will not come loose when the motor is working.

▲ Push the knitting needle into the centre of the cork. If there is already a hole in the cork, fill up the space with plasticine to make a tight fit. Make sure there are about 5 cm. of knitting needle sticking out of each side.

▲ Wind 80-90 turns of fine wire round the cork. Stick in two pins (see 9 below) which should be the same distance from the shaft. If you find this difficult, stick the pins into the cork before winding on the wire.

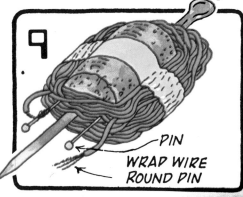

9 PIN
WRAP WIRE ROUND PIN

10 FOLD OVER
5 cm.

11 PINS
DRAWING PIN
BRUSHES SHOULD TOUCH PINS LIKE THIS

▲ Remove 4 cm. of insulation from the loose ends of the wire. Wind one of the bare wires round a pin. Repeat for the other wire and pin. Make sure they are firmly in place. Place the shaft on its crossed-pin supports.

▲ Take two 30 cm. lengths of the thicker wire. Remove the insulation from one end of each wire for a distance of about 5 cm. Place half a milk bottle top over the end and fold it over to make a 5 cm. long strip.

▲ Pin the thicker wires to the baseboard so that the flexible bottle top brushes touch the pins at the same instant when the shaft turns. These wires will be connected to the batteries when the motor is ready to run.

12 MAKE SURE POLES OF MAGNETS ARE LIKE THIS
N   S

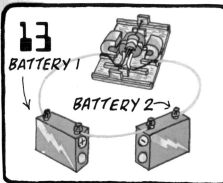

13 BATTERY 1
BATTERY 2

14 Troubleshooting!

▲ Place the magnets in position. Make sure that the two poles facing each other are opposite poles (test this by seeing that they attract one another). The armature should lie directly between the two poles.

Connect the ⊕ of battery 1 to the ⊖ of battery 2 with the third length of wire. Then connect the brush wires to the ⊖ of battery 1 and the ⊕ of battery 2. A gentle push should start the motor spinning round.

No matter how much care you take, your motor might not work first time. Points to check are:

1. Make sure the armature is free to turn.
2. Keep the magnets as close as possible to, but not touching, the armature.
3. When the armature is horizontal it should lie between the poles of the magnets.
4. Make sure the brushes touch the pins at exactly the same instant.
5. The brushes should just stroke the pins as they pass.

HOW ELECTRIC MOTORS ARE USED

▲ This Boeing jetliner uses electric motors to spin the giant turbines as the engines are started, and electric blowers de-ice the windscreen and work the air conditioning.

Electricity is used to drive all sorts of things—from huge locomotives to electric clocks.

The combination of great power and high precision has led to the widespread use of electric motors in the home as well as in factories.

You will probably be surprised at the number of gadgets in your home that use motors. Try making a check list of all the things in your house that have one.

▲ The vacuum cleaner is a useful tool in the home. The motor turns a high speed fan which produces a suction effect in the flexible pipe. Dust and dirt sucked in are trapped in a disposable paper bag.

▲ The motor shown here is lifting sweets from a conveyor belt into a container that weighs out the right quantity and packs them automatically. The motor lifts over 100,000 sweets every day. That's a lot of sweets!

▲ As motor-cycles get bigger, the old fashioned kick starter is being replaced by an electric starter motor like those used in motor cars. The rider simply presses a button on the handlebars to set the engine going.

▲ Manufacturers have to use more and more motors to speed up production in factories. In this picture aerosol cans full of fly killer are passed along a motor-driven belt ready to have their labels stuck on.

▲ Motor-driven machines can do many jobs much better and faster than people. All the pages in this book were stitched together by machines like the one above. If you look carefully, you can see this page in the picture above.

ALTERNATING CURRENT

The electricity supplied by a battery flows in one direction and is called direct current.

The other sort of electricity, made in power stations, is called alternating current. The electrons move to and fro in the wire instead of in one direction. But they produce the same effect as electrons drifting only one way.

▶ To make alternating current, power stations use generators that have coils like an electric motor. As each coil is turned between the two magnets, current is made—the exact opposite of an electric motor. But the amount of current varies as the coil turns round.

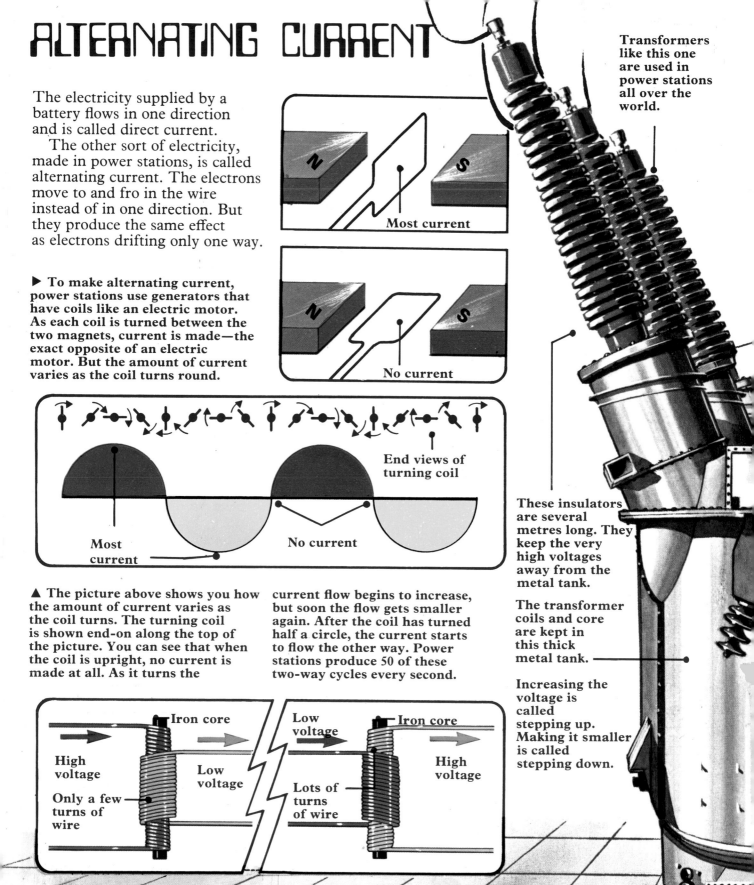

Most current

No current

End views of turning coil

Most current

No current

▲ The picture above shows you how the amount of current varies as the coil turns. The turning coil is shown end-on along the top of the picture. You can see that when the coil is upright, no current is made at all. As it turns the current flow begins to increase, but soon the flow gets smaller again. After the coil has turned half a circle, the current starts to flow the other way. Power stations produce 50 of these two-way cycles every second.

Iron core

High voltage

Low voltage

Only a few turns of wire

Low voltage

Iron core

High voltage

Lots of turns of wire

▲ Alternating current is useful because its voltage can be changed by using a transformer, which is simply two coils of insulated wire wound round an iron core. Although there is no electrical connection between the two coils, any voltage in the first coil sets up a voltage in the second coil. This effect is called induction. Larger or smaller voltages—whatever is needed—can be set up by varying the number of turns in the two coils.

Transformers like this one are used in power stations all over the world.

These insulators are several metres long. They keep the very high voltages away from the metal tank.

The transformer coils and core are kept in this thick metal tank.

Increasing the voltage is called stepping up. Making it smaller is called stepping down.

High voltage power lines enter and leave the transformer through large insulators.

Oil flows round the coils keeping them cool.

How induction works

The current flow in a transformer's second coil is set up by a magnetic effect called induction. Induction only works when a current is getting bigger or smaller, not when it is a steady flow. This is why power stations use alternating current which varies all the time as the coils in a generator spin round. Turn your battery on and off to provide the varying current you need.

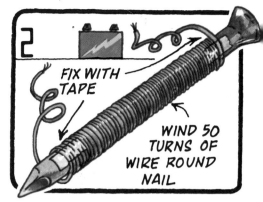

2 FIX WITH TAPE. WIND 50 TURNS OF WIRE ROUND NAIL

▲ You will need a large nail and enough wire to make 100 turns of wire round it. Cut the wire in half and wind 50 turns round the nail. Use sticky tape to stop it unwinding. Leave 10 cm. of wire free at each end.

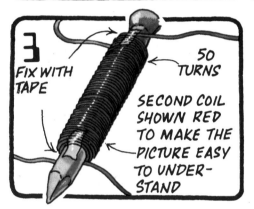

3 FIX WITH TAPE. 50 TURNS. SECOND COIL SHOWN RED TO MAKE THE PICTURE EASY TO UNDERSTAND

▲ Wind the rest of the wire over the top of the first coil. Tape it down so it does not unwind. Leave about 1 m. of wire free at the ends of this coil. Strip off 2 cm. of insulation from the ends of the two coils.

4 NORTH. 30 TURNS

▲ More wire and a compass needed! Wind 30 turns round the compass and tape it firmly. The wire coil should line up with the compass needle. The needle will kick sideways when any electric current flows in the wire round it.

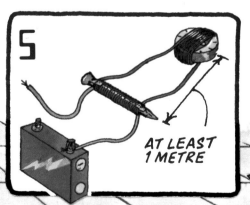

5 AT LEAST 1 METRE

▲ Connect the compass wires to the second coil wires. Make sure the compass is 1 m. away from the coil. This is because the compass might point towards the nail when you switch the current from the battery on.

6 TAPE COMPASS TO TABLE. COMPASS WILL KICK, THEN SINK BACK. KICK AGAIN WHEN YOU SWITCH OFF

▲ Connect a wire to one of the battery terminals. Touch the other wire to the other terminal. The needle will kick, then sink back. Switch off and the needle will kick again in the other direction.

INSIDE A POWER STATION

Although electricity appears naturally as lightning, it is impossible to turn this to our own use. Even if the power of lightning could be used there is no way to know when or where it would strike.

The electricity used for lighting, warming homes and running industry is completely man-made.

It is difficult to store large amounts of electricity, so power stations are designed to produce electricity at the time that it is needed.

▲ Power stations use turbine wheels (which are rather like propellers on a ship) to turn the coils in their generators. One way to spin turbines is to use fast flowing water, so rivers are dammed to provide the water.

▲ Most power stations use coal or oil. The fuel burns and boils water. The steam from the boiling water is passed through pipes to spin turbines which turn the generator coils. Most modern power stations are very clean.

A giant turbine generator

Power stations burn coal or oil, or use nuclear fuel, to heat water up to make high pressure steam. The steam spins turbines, and a generator attached to the turbine shaft produces hundreds of megawatts of electricity. A megawatt is a million watts—enough to light 10,000 powerful light bulbs.

1 Steam produced by the boiler is fed into cylinders containing the turbines.

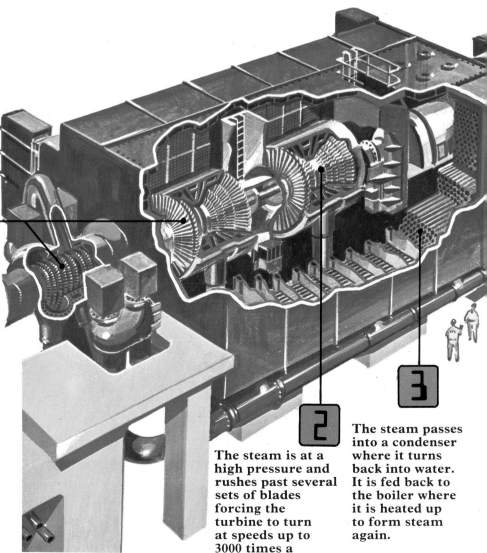

2 The steam is at a high pressure and rushes past several sets of blades forcing the turbine to turn at speeds up to 3000 times a minute.

3 The steam passes into a condenser where it turns back into water. It is fed back to the boiler where it is heated up to form steam again.

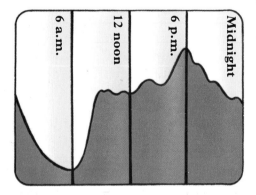

▲ This chart shows when power is most needed. There is a steep increase in the morning as people wake up and put on the kettle at breakfast time. There is another peak at 6 p.m. when they return from work.

▲ The power behind the atom bomb can be used peacefully, and nuclear power stations are producing more and more of the world's electricity. But one problem is the dangerous radioactive waste produced.

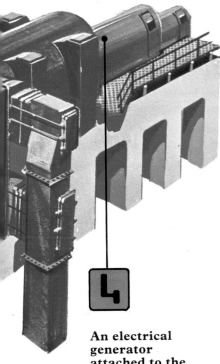

An electrical generator attached to the end of the turbine shaft turns round with it and produces power.

1 Make a spinning turbine wheel

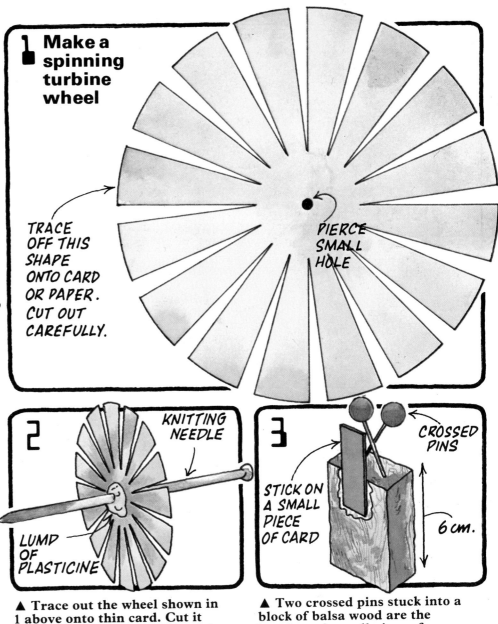

TRACE OFF THIS SHAPE ONTO CARD OR PAPER. CUT OUT CAREFULLY.

PIERCE SMALL HOLE

2
KNITTING NEEDLE

LUMP OF PLASTICINE

▲ Trace out the wheel shown in 1 above onto thin card. Cut it out, and pierce the middle with a knitting needle as shown here. Fix two lumps of plasticine on either side to keep it steady, otherwise it will not work.

3
CROSSED PINS

STICK ON A SMALL PIECE OF CARD

6 cm.

▲ Two crossed pins stuck into a block of balsa wood are the bearings. A small piece of card stuck on the back will stop the needle sliding through the crossed pins. Make two sets of bearings.

4
BEND BLADES

▲ Carefully twist each of the blades at a small angle. This will make the turbine spin round when you blow through it. You will have to experiment to find the angle which will spin the wheel round fast.

5
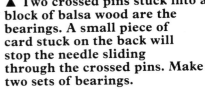
BLOW GENTLY

FIX WITH PLASTICINE

▲ Place the balsa blocks on a table. Place the needle on the crossed-pin bearings. Using your breath just like the steam in a power station, blow along the needle. The turbine will spin round just like the real thing.

POWER LINES ACROSS THE COUNTRY

Cooling towers

Power station produces electricity at 11,000 volts.

1

Transformers increase the voltage to 400,000 volts for transmission around the country.

2

The pylons on a 400,000 volt overhead line are 50 m. high.

Factory

Many of the things we take for granted every day, like switching on a light or boiling water in a kettle, would be impossible without a safe and reliable supply of electricity.

Electricity cannot be stored easily and so the generators at power stations work 24 hours a day to produce electricity as and when it is needed.

From the power station a complicated network of overhead lines and underground cables brings the power to your home.

The numbers on this big picture match up with the numbers in the boxes below.

▲ Power station generators make electricity at 11,000 volts. To deliver electricity with as little waste as possible a very high voltage must be used. So transformers at the station step up the voltage to 400,000 volts.

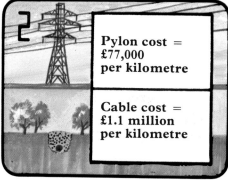

Pylon cost = £77,000 per kilometre

Cable cost = £1.1 million per kilometre

▲ Electricity can be carried over the countryside on overhead lines or underground cables. Pylons over the ground are ugly but they are much cheaper to make and erect than underground cables as you can see above.

▲ When lightning strikes an overhead line, switches called circuit breakers cut off that section of the line. Users on the 'dead' part are left without electricity until the fault is put right.

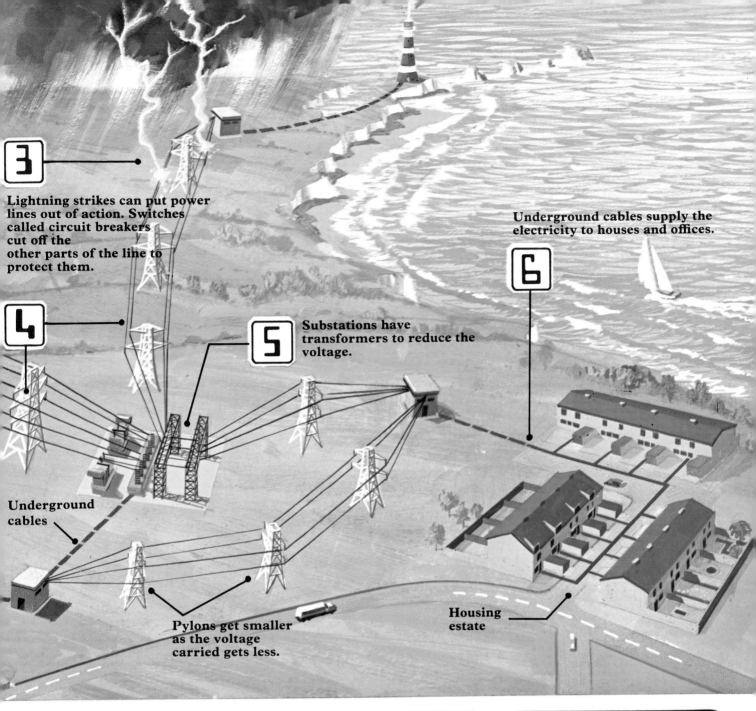

3 Lightning strikes can put power lines out of action. Switches called circuit breakers cut off the other parts of the line to protect them.

4

5 Substations have transformers to reduce the voltage.

6 Underground cables supply the electricity to houses and offices.

Underground cables

Pylons get smaller as the voltage carried gets less.

Housing estate

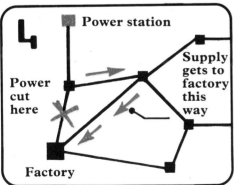

4 Power station

Power cut here

Supply gets to factory this way

Factory

▲ To avoid power cuts caused by lightning, electricity supply lines are arranged in an inter-connecting grid. If one of the supplies to a factory is cut off, it can still get its supply from another line.

5

▲ When the electricity reaches the main substation, it is still at a very high voltage. Step-down transformers in the substation reduce the voltage to a lower level which is carried on smaller, lighter pylons.

6

▲ The final link in the chain from power station to home. Underground cables are used in towns because overhead lines would be dangerous. They pass beneath the pavement and feed the power to your home.

INSIDE THE HOME

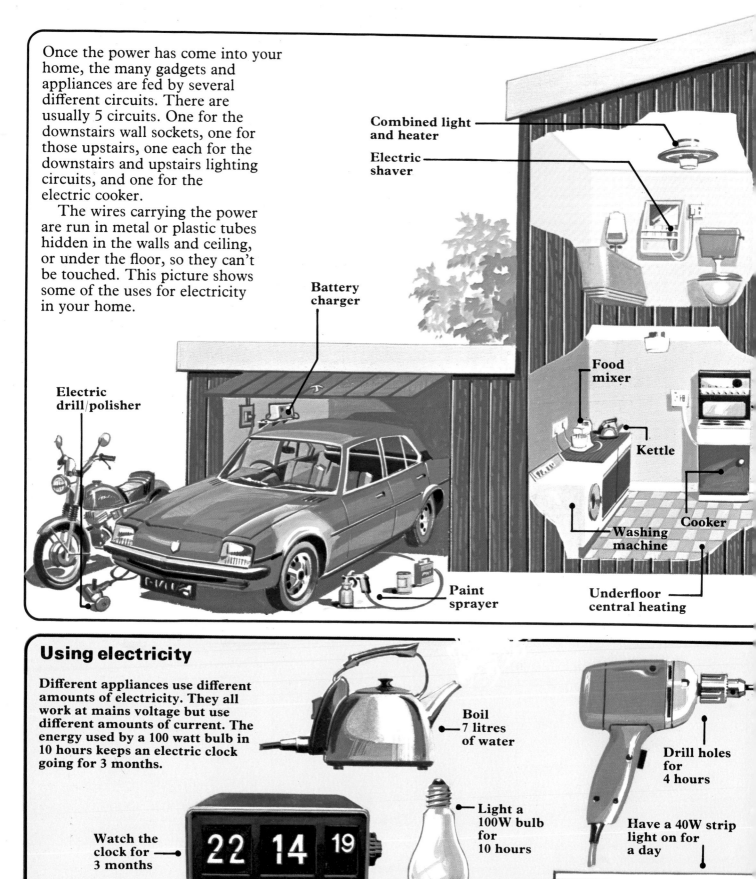

Once the power has come into your home, the many gadgets and appliances are fed by several different circuits. There are usually 5 circuits. One for the downstairs wall sockets, one for those upstairs, one each for the downstairs and upstairs lighting circuits, and one for the electric cooker.

The wires carrying the power are run in metal or plastic tubes hidden in the walls and ceiling, or under the floor, so they can't be touched. This picture shows some of the uses for electricity in your home.

Combined light and heater

Electric shaver

Battery charger

Food mixer

Kettle

Electric drill/polisher

Cooker

Washing machine

Paint sprayer

Underfloor central heating

Using electricity

Different appliances use different amounts of electricity. They all work at mains voltage but use different amounts of current. The energy used by a 100 watt bulb in 10 hours keeps an electric clock going for 3 months.

Boil 7 litres of water

Drill holes for 4 hours

Watch the clock for 3 months

22 14 19

Light a 100W bulb for 10 hours

Have a 40W strip light on for a day

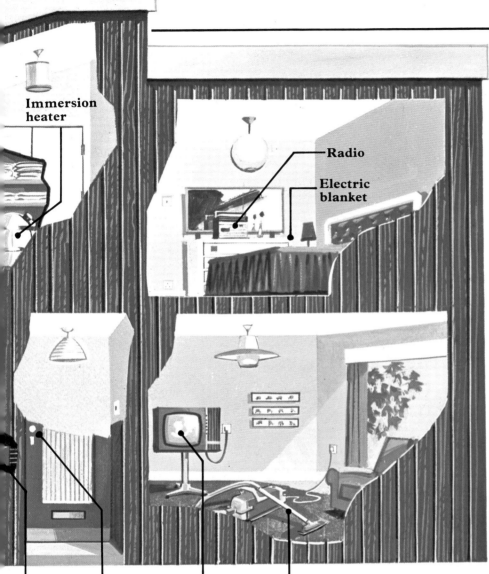

Immersion heater

Radio

Electric blanket

Fuse box

Doorbell

Television

Vacuum cleaner

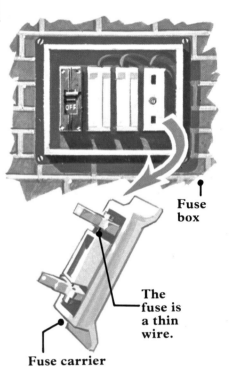

Fuse box

The fuse is a thin wire.

Fuse carrier

▲ The current flow to each circuit in a house passes through a fuse, which is a strand of wire held in a plastic carrier. If a fault in the circuit makes a high current flow, the fuse heats up and breaks, cutting off the power supply.

The fault must then be put right and the fuse replaced.

Some new houses have circuit breakers instead of fuses to cut off the power supply.

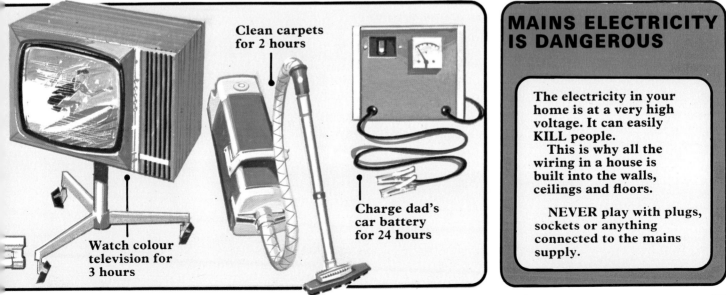

Clean carpets for 2 hours

Charge dad's car battery for 24 hours

Watch colour television for 3 hours

MAINS ELECTRICITY IS DANGEROUS

The electricity in your home is at a very high voltage. It can easily KILL people.

This is why all the wiring in a house is built into the walls, ceilings and floors.

NEVER play with plugs, sockets or anything connected to the mains supply.

TELEGRAPH AND TELEPHONE

The invention of the electric telegraph in 1838 enabled people to communicate directly with one another over long distances. The only connection between then was the wire which carried the message.

Before Bell invented the telephone in 1876 it was not possible to talk over a telegraph wire. So the message had to be coded into a series of long and short electrical currents which were passed along the wire and decoded at the receiving station. This is why a telegram is sometimes called a 'wire'.

▲ You will need two 4.5 volt batteries, two 6 volt bulbs in holders, a sheet of cardboard and a sheet of cooking foil. Decide where to put the two telegraph stations. Get enough 3-core flex to join the two.

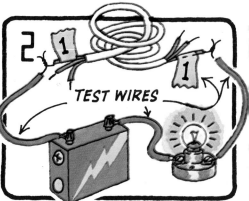

▲ To find out which wire is which, wire up a battery and bulb as shown. Connect a test wire to one of the flex wires. Touch the other wires until the bulb glows. Mark the wires and repeat for the others.

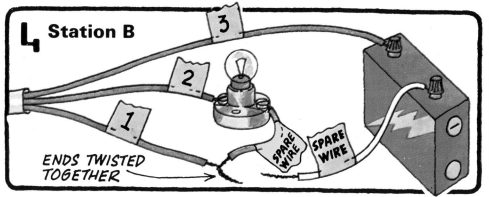

Station B

ENDS TWISTED TOGETHER

SPARE WIRE SPARE WIRE

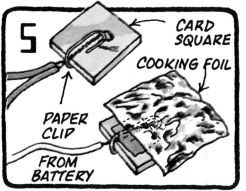

CARD SQUARE

COOKING FOIL

PAPER CLIP

FROM BATTERY

▲ To make station B, wire 3 of the flex's other end is connected to the ⊕ terminal of the other battery. Wire 2 is connected to the other bulbholder. Join the holder's other terminal to wire 1 with a spare wire. Fix the other spare wire to the battery ⊖ terminal. Double-check all the connections you have made so far, to avoid mistakes—the wiring is quite complicated and if you make a mistake, you might have to start all over again!

▲ You need four Morse tappers. One on each of the spare wires from a battery, and one on each pair of twisted-together wires. Clip the wires to squares of cardboard with paper clips, and glue cooking foil over the top.

A century of telephones

"Mr. Watson, come here, I want to see you." Alexander Graham Bell's historic call to his assistant in 1876 was the first time speech had been transmitted over a wire.

Bell realised the importance of his new invention and set up a telephone company to satisfy the sudden demand for telephones.

Within two years of this first demonstration thousands of telephones had been installed in offices in America, and within five years Bell retired from the business a famous and wealthy man.

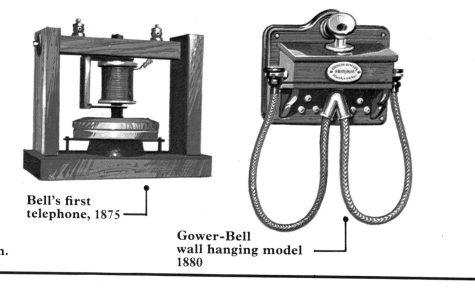

Bell's first telephone, 1875

Gower-Bell wall hanging model 1880

Before messages can be sent over a telegraph wire they must be coded into electrical signals at the sending end. In the code invented by Samuel Morse the 26 letters of the alphabet are represented by 26 different combinations of long and short dots and dashes. Remember that to be exact, your dashes should be three times as long as your dots.

3 Station A

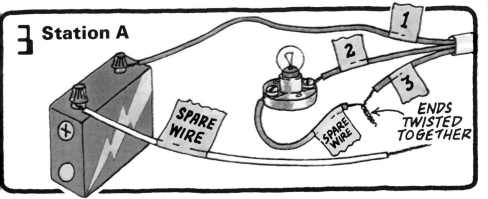

▲ To make station A, attach wire 1 from the flex to the ⊖ terminal of a battery. Connect wire 2 to a bulbholder. Connect a piece of spare wire to the bulbholder's other terminal, twisting its other end with wire 3.

The second spare wire should be attached to the battery's ⊕ terminal. Remember that these details are to show you how to wire up the telegraph system properly. The wire lengths depend on where you put the stations.

▲ Fix each bulbholder and one of the tappers to a sheet of card that will hang on the wall of Station A. Do the same for Station B. It's a good idea to have a pad of paper there too to write down messages as they come

in. Unless you already know the Morse Code, you will need to use the one we have printed here to code any message you want to send, or to decode messages that come in. Once you get the hang of it, see how fast you can decode Morse!

Table model 1920's

Push button model 1970's

21st CENTURY ELECTRICITY

If we go on using coal, oil and gas as fast as we do now, they will be used up in under 100 years. So scientists are looking for other ways of producing electricity.

One idea shown here is for an orbiting solar collector that turns sunlight into electricity and then sends it down to Earth.

Another possibility is a nuclear fusion reactor. The fuels needed for fusion are found in sea water, so the world's oceans could one day produce almost limitless supplies of energy.

The solar collector picks up the sunlight and converts it into electricity using solar cells like the ones which power many of today's satellites. The bigger it is the more electricity it produces. This one measures 8 km. by 8 km. which is as large as 13,000 football pitches.

The Sun

Sun's rays caught by the collector.

The sunlight reaching the Earth's surface has been filtered through the atmosphere, but the solar collector out in space catches all the direct rays of the Sun. It produces far more electricity out in space than it would do on Earth.

The power transmitter is connected to the solar collector, and the pair orbit the Earth. They stay in orbit above the receiving station on the Earth's surface 35,880 km. below.

Superspeed railways

The 21st century railway train will be very different from today's model. It will be driven by linear electric motors and will glide along a track at speeds up to 400 k.p.h. Wheels will not be used because the train will be suspended a few centimetres above the track by powerful magnetic fields.

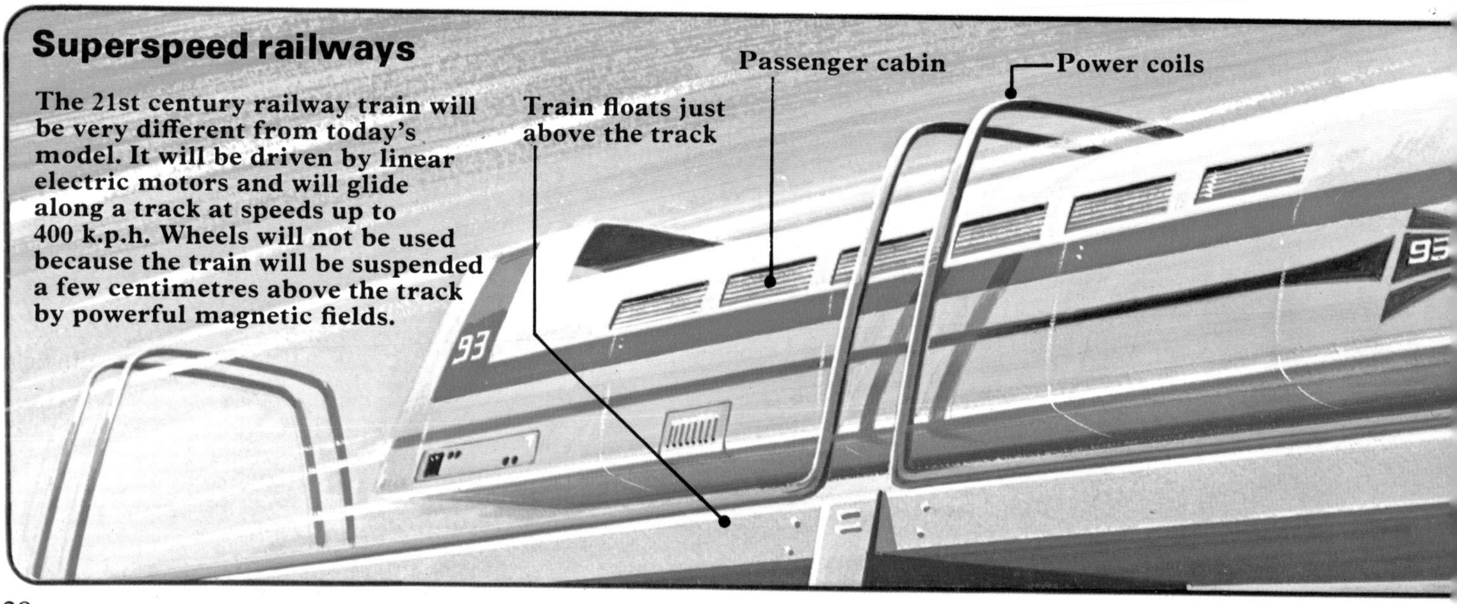

Passenger cabin

Power coils

Train floats just above the track

Power beam to Earth

To collect the power beamed down from the orbiting collector, a large collecting area is needed. Each receiving station collects enough power to supply one major city with electricity.

Driver's cabin

Power from the atom

Today's atomic power stations are all fission reactors. Atoms are split in the reactor and the heat given off is used to boil water for steam. Fission reactors have one major problem—radioactive waste. So scientists are trying to make fusion reactors. A fusion reactor would have little or no dangerous waste.

▶ Fusion is the combining of atoms of deuterium and tritium—both found in sea water. When the two atoms join they give off a lot of energy as heat, which can be used to produce electricity.

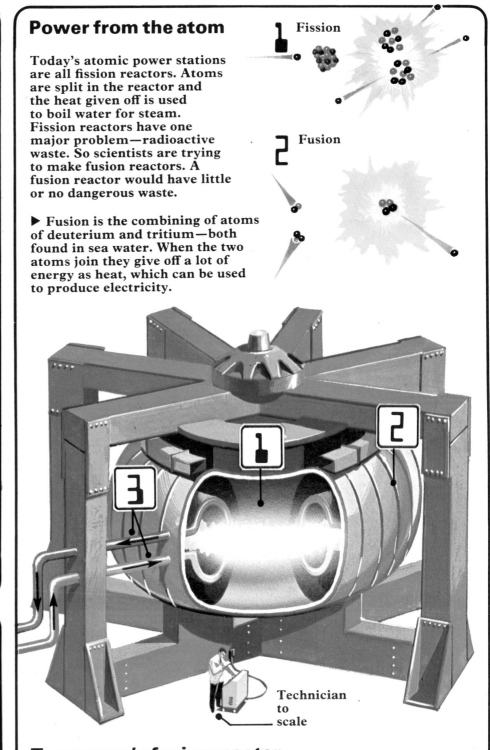

1 Fission

2 Fusion

Technician to scale

Tomorrow's fusion reactor

▲ Deuterium and tritium atoms join only at a temperature of 100 million°C. No known material will withstand such a high temperature and the only suitable container for the reaction is a powerful magnetic field (1). The field is produced by a huge electric current flowing through coils of wire embedded in the doughnut-shaped concrete wall (2). Lithium—a metal liquefied by the heat—is pumped through pipes (3) to boil water. The steam given off turns turbines, which turn the coils in a generator.

ELECTRIC FIRSTS

Here are some of the milestones in the development of modern electricity. You will see that some of the inventions have become such an accepted part of day to day routine that it is difficult to imagine what life would be like without them.

Edison's electric lamp

1600
English scientist William Gilbert published his theory that the Earth had a magnetic field.

1672
Otto von Guericke invented the first electrical machine. A large sulphur ball turned by a handle produced static electricity when a hand was rubbed against it.

1752
Benjamin Franklin showed that thunderclouds are charged with static electricity.

1800
The first electric battery was made by Count Alessandro Volta in Italy.

1831
English scientist Michael Faraday built the first generator of electric current.

1837
The first electric telegraph was built by Samuel Morse in America. The code that bears his name is still used today.

1858
The first transatlantic telegraph cable was laid.

1876
Scottish born inventor Alexander Graham Bell invented the telephone.

1879
The world's first electric railway was opened in Berlin.

Thomas Edison made the first electric light bulb. It glowed for 40 hours before the filament burned out.

1882
Edison set up the first public electricity supply. His Pearl Street station in New York supplied power to shops and houses over an area of 2 square kilometres.

1956
The first power station to produce electricity from the power of the atom was opened at Calder Hall, England. There are now more than 300 nuclear power stations all over the world.

1975
The first production-line built electric car rolled off the assembly line.

Copper disc

Magnet

Faraday's electric generator

ELECTRIC FACTS

Electricity can be our willing servant or our deadly enemy. It can light an electric lamp or produce a killer thunderbolt. Here are some facts about electricity and how it is used.

The world's biggest power station came into service in 1970 on the Yenisei River in Siberia. It is a hydroelectric station producing more than 6 million kW of power, and the reservoir behind the dam is over 380 km. long. The U.S.S.R. also uses the highest voltages for power transmission. In some areas power lines work at 800,000 volts.

Japan's bullet train

The world speed record for a train running on an ordinary railway track is held by an electric locomotive. In March 1955 the train reached a speed of 330 k.p.h. in France. Electric trains on the Tokaido line in Japan regularly reach top speeds of 255 k.p.h.

The newest transatlantic telephone cable is very thin. It is less than 4 cm. in diameter and can carry more than 1800 telephone calls at the same time. Old fashioned cables had to be very thick to do this.

There are more than 400 million telephones throughout the world. People in some countries can dial direct to as many as 26 others without an operator having to connect the call for them.

The latest communications satellite links Europe, Africa and America. It can relay up to 6000 telephone calls at the same time.

In a modern nuclear power station, 1 kg. of uranium fuel produces as much electricity as 2000 tonnes of coal in a conventional station. When the problems of nuclear fusion are solved, 1 kg. of fuel will produce six times as much electricity again.

The filament of an electric light bulb is made of tungsten, which is one of the best heat resisting materials known. It will withstand temperatures up to 3400°C before melting.

If we could convert into electricity the sunlight falling on a 200 km. square of the Sahara desert, there would be enough power to supply every country in the world with electricity.

The body's nervous system depends on tiny electric currents to pass messages from sense organs to the brain and out again to the muscles. These currents travel at speeds up to 400 km. per hour.

The most powerful flashes of lightning contain enough energy to power a small village for a day. The temperature within the bolt itself is about 30,000°C. The temperature on the surface of the Sun is only 6000°C.

The world's tallest electricity pylons are used to carry power from Italy across the Straits of Messina to Sicily. The pylons tower 220 m. into the air (taller than a fifty storey office block). The distance between the pylons is 3.6 km.

ELECTRIC WORDS

Here is a list of some of the technical words used in the book. You will find only those words that were not fully explained on the pages where they appeared.

Armature
The coils in an electric motor that are forced to spin round by the magnetic fields.

Brushes
Conducting pads in an electric motor that pass current to the spinning armature.

Circuit
A path along which electric current travels. Current will not flow until the circuit is complete.

Conductor
A material that allows electric current to flow through it easily.

Condenser
In a power station steam from the turbines is passed into the condenser where it is turned back into water.

Electrodes
The two rods that carry current into and out of the electrolyte in a battery.

Electrolyte
The liquid or paste in a battery. Chemical changes in it produce electricity.

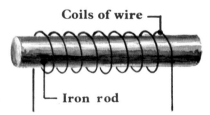

Coils of wire

Iron rod

Electromagnet
An iron rod with many coils of wire wrapped round it. When current is passed through the coils, the iron becomes a very powerful magnet.

Fission
The splitting of uranium atoms by shooting neutrons at them. As the atoms split they release energy that can be turned into electricity.

Fusion
The joining up of two atoms. A lot of energy is given off as they combine.

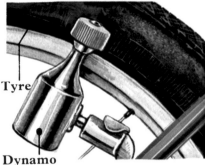

Tyre

Dynamo

Generator
A machine that produces electric current as it spins round. Generators in power stations produce a.c. Generators that produce only direct current are called dynamos. Bicycles often have a dynamo on the back wheel to power the front and rear lights.

Insulator
Any material that does not allow electricity to flow through it.

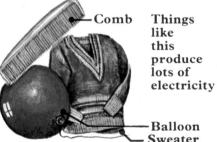

Comb — Things like this produce lots of electricity

Balloon
Sweater

Static electricity
The form of electricity produced when some materials are rubbed together.

Substation
An electricity station where a transformer reduces the voltage of the electricity supply.

Switch
A switch controls the flow of electric current. When the switch is off the circuit is broken and the current flow stops.

Transformer
A device used for increasing or reducing a voltage. Transformers work only with alternating current.

CIRCUITS AND SWITCHES

The experiments in the book have had pictures of bulbs, batteries and so on to show you how to connect them up. But when complicated circuits are drawn it is easier to use symbols. Connect up the circuits on this page using the list of symbols shown on the right.

See the effect of putting a switch in another part of the circuit; check how brightly bulbs glow when two are used instead of one. When you have done these, you can try designing some circuits of your own.

What the signs and symbols mean

———— Wire

Connection between wires

+ ― Battery

Light bulb

Switch

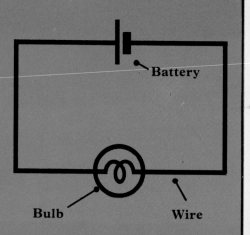

Battery

Bulb **Wire**

The simplest circuit is a bulb connected to a battery. There must be a wire to take the current out of the battery to the bulb, and another to return it to the battery.

Making a switch

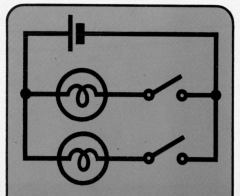

PAPERCLIP   WOOD BLOCK

To help you use these other circuits, you need to make this switch. You need two drawing pins, a small block of wood and a paperclip. Make it up as shown in the picture.

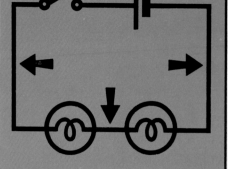

Here the bulbs are connected 'in series'. When the switch is off current will not flow. Try connecting the switch in the other places arrowed. Does it still work?

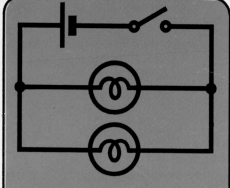

This is a 'parallel' circuit. You can see that when the circuit is completed by turning the switch on, both bulbs are controlled by it.

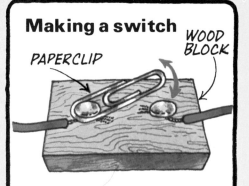

This circuit is very like the one before, but two switches are in the circuit instead of one. How many bulbs does each switch control when you turn it on?

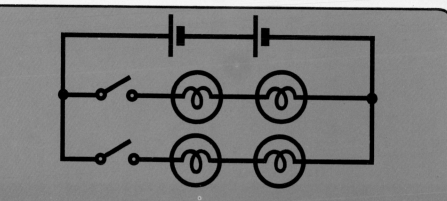

It is possible to connect batteries in series or parallel too—just like the bulbs earlier on. But remember to connect the ⊖ of the first battery to the ⊕ of the second. This means that the voltage in the circuit is twice that of each 4.5 volt battery, making a total of 9 volts. Each switch in this circuit controls two of the four light bulbs.